TIME HOP SWEETS SHOP

Sundaes with Harriet Tubman

By Kyla Steinkraus

Illustrated by Sally Garland

Rourke
Educational Media
rourkeeducationalmedia.com

www.rourkeeducationalmedia.com

Edited by: Keli Sipperley
Cover and Interior layout by: Tara Raymo
Cover and Interior Illustrations by: Sally Garland

Library of Congress PCN Data

Sundaes with Harriet Tubman / Kyla Steinkraus
(Time Hop Sweets Shop)
ISBN (hard cover)(alk. paper) 978-1-68191-371-1
ISBN (soft cover) 978-1-68191-413-8
ISBN (e-Book) 978-1-68191-454-1
Library of Congress Control Number: 2015951483

Printed in the United States of America,
North Mankato, Minnesota

Dear Parents and Teachers,

Fiona and Finley are just like any modern-day kids. They help out with the family business, face struggles and triumphs at school, travel through time with important historical figures ...

Well, maybe that part's not so ordinary. At the Time Hop Sweets Shop, anything can happen, at any point in time. The family bakery draws customers from all over the map—and all over the history books. And when Tick Tock the parrot squawks, Fiona and Finley know an adventure is about to begin!

These beginner chapter books are designed to introduce students to important people in U.S. history, turning their accomplishments into adventures that Fiona, Finley, and young readers get to experience right along with them.

Perfect as read-alouds, read-alongs, or independent readers, books in the Time Hop Sweets Shop series were written to delight, inform, and engage your child or students by making each historical figure memorable and relatable. Each book includes a biography, comprehension questions, websites for further reading, and more.

We look forward to our time travels together!

Happy Reading,
Rourke Educational Media

Table of Contents

A Dark Time in History

It was a sad and rainy day outside. The sky was gray. Inside the Sweets Shop, Finley felt sad and gray himself.

Usually Finley and his sister Fiona loved helping Mom and Dad after school. They made all kinds of cakes, cookies, and candies.

The Sweets Shop was special because it had desserts from different time periods, like Washington cake, tea cake cookies, and of course, green tomato pie.

"What's wrong?" Fiona asked. She was refilling the chocolate sauce container. Somehow a whole bunch of chocolate ended up all over her hands and face. She licked her fingers.

Even though she was a whole year younger than Finley, she was just as tall. She thought this made her the boss all the time. Finley was sure it didn't.

"Your face looks like a thundercloud, Fin," Mom said. She was making her famous flaky pie crusts. "Do you want to talk about it?"

Finley sighed. "I like school almost all the time. But today in Social Studies class, we learned about something terrible. Our teacher told us about slavery."

"What is slavery?" Fiona asked.

Mom put down her rolling pin. "Slavery is terrible. If you were a slave, you were owned by another person. You were treated like property. You worked long hours without pay. You were beaten with a whip if you made a mistake. The slave owner could sell your mother or your brother or sister any time he wished. If he sold you, you would never see your family again."

"That's awful!" Fiona said. "What country

did such terrible things?"

"Our country," Mom said softly. "Before the Civil War, the southern states allowed black people to be enslaved. In most of the northern states, slavery was illegal."

Fiona felt angry and sad at the same time. "How could anybody do that?" she whispered.

"I don't know," Mom said. "It was a dark time in our history. But still, there were many people who believed slavery was wrong. Some people even risked their own lives to help slaves escape to freedom."

Finley's eyes brightened. "Really?"

"Yes. But I'm not sure if I'm the best person to talk about this." Mom looked at the side door.

Tick Tock, the family's parrot, ruffled his feathers on his perch. "Look at the time! Look at the time!" he squawked.

Fiona and Finley grinned at each other. A special visitor was coming!

The bell over the side door jingled as a small African American woman walked in. She wore a long, dark dress with a scarf covering her head. Her shoulders were hunched over as she shuffled to the counter. She looked very old.

"Hello! Can we help you?" Finley asked.

The visitor straightened her shoulders and looked up with a smile. Suddenly she wasn't old at all!

Fiona gasped. "How did you do that?"

"It is amazing how people will think you are old, if you act like it," the woman said. "Acting like an old lady was one of my many disguises!"

"Wowza," Fiona said.

"Now, could I get a vanilla ice cream sundae? I never had anything sweet as a child. I'm making up for it now!" The woman sat down at the counter.

Finley scooped the ice cream into a glass dish. Fiona poured on the chocolate sauce and whipped cream. Then Finley topped it with some sprinkles and a cherry.

"This is wonderful!" The woman said. "Just what I need before I get back to conducting my train."

"Do you work on a railroad?" Finley asked.

"Sort of." The woman smiled. "It isn't a railroad that you can see. I use it to save my people."

"You mean the Underground Railroad!" Finley said. "We started learning about that in school. You must be Harriet Tubman!"

The woman nodded. "That's me!"

"What in the world is an Underground Railroad?" Fiona asked. She imagined a train rumbling through tunnels deep under the earth.

Harriet took a big bite of ice cream. "The Underground Railroad was a secret group of people who helped runaway slaves escape to freedom in Canada, where slavery

was illegal. Each home was a station that we traveled to. The runaways were called passengers. And I was a conductor! People like me guided the runaways along the entire journey."

Fiona frowned. "Were you a slave?"

"Yes," Harriet said. "I was forced to work all day when I was only five years old. I had to work even when I was very sick. If my owners didn't think I worked hard enough, they would whip me."

"That's terrible," Finley said. "Is that how you got that scar on your forehead?"

Harriet shook her head. "When I was twelve, a slave master threw a heavy weight at my head. I was unconscious for days. I still get bad headaches and I fall asleep at strange times. But I never let anything stop me. I escaped from slavery when I was twenty-two. I walked over ninety miles through swamps and woods to freedom."

"Wowza," Fiona whispered.

"That is just the beginning." Harriet smiled. "How would you like to come with me to the year 1856? It is November, and I am conducting a group of runaway slaves on a very dangerous journey."

"Yes! Yes!" Finley and Fiona cried.

Mom gave them each a hug. "Be brave!"

They followed Harriet to the side door of the Sweets Shop.

"See you soon!" Tick Tock cawed as the Sweets Shop began to whirl and shake.

A Dangerous Journey

It felt like they were spinning in a washing machine!

Finley turned a sickly shade of green.

"Oh!" he moaned as he landed hard on the ground.

"Wasn't that fun?" Fiona said, elbowing him.

"Not at all." Finley brushed off his clothes, which had changed in the time hop. He was wearing pants with a white cotton shirt. Fiona wore a long dark dress with a white collar.

The night air was sharp and cold. The sky was scattered with stars. Dark tree branches swayed above them. Finley wrapped his arms around himself.

"Who are they?" someone whispered.

Harriet patted Fiona's shoulder. "They are friends. They will help us." She introduced Fiona and Finley to three men named Joe, Bill, and Peter, and a woman named Eliza.

Finley turned up his hearing aids so he could hear the whispering.

"Why do we need to be quiet?" Fiona asked in her softest voice. It was very hard for her to be so quiet. She liked to be loud.

Harriet parted the bushes with her hands. They saw a road just ahead that led to a bridge with many dark figures standing on it. Fiona could see the shape of guns in the moonlight.

"We need to cross the Delaware Bridge," Harriet said. "There's no other way around it."

"But it's guarded!" Finley said.

"There are slave catchers and police on that bridge," Joe said. "They catch runaway slaves. They want to catch me especially. I am very valuable to my owner. He put up reward posters everywhere."

"I've got my own reward posters," Harriet said with a grin. "Don't you worry. I have a plan. We will have to cross in disguise."

Harriet led them back through the woods. She took them to a small white house, one of the stations of the Underground Railroad. A lantern glowed on the porch. The runaways hid while Finley knocked on the front door. A woman answered in her nightgown.

Finley's heart thumped wildly in his chest. What if they were at the wrong house? "A friend with friends," he whispered.

The woman looked at him. Then she smiled. "Welcome! Please, bring in your friends."

Harriet left the group at the house while she went to work out her plan.

The kind woman led the group to her attic.
She gave them bread and soup to eat. "It is
a dangerous time," she said quietly. "The
slave catchers are everywhere. Be careful."

"What happens if you get caught?" Fiona
asked Joe.

"They will take us back to our owners,"
Joe said. "We could be beaten, put in jail, or
even killed."

"And the lady who helped us? What would happen to her?" Finley asked. His whole body felt cold with fear.

Joe shook his head. "She would go to prison for many years."

"The people who run the Underground Railroad are very brave," Fiona said.

Soon Harriet returned. She had a bricklayer's wagon. The back of the wagon was full of bricks. "We will hide underneath the bricks," she said. "Fiona and Finley, will you ride with the driver? You must be a distraction, so the police do not think to stop the wagon."

Fiona and Finley nodded. They climbed onto the wagon.

"Stop shaking!" Fiona hissed.

"But I'm scared!" Finley said. "What if—"

Harriet put her hand on Finley's arm. "Have faith, my boy. We will not fail."

A Thrilling Escape

The driver handed Finley the reins. "Are we ready?"

Finley took a deep breath. It was time to be brave! "Yes, sir!"

They drove back up the road to the bridge. Even in the chilly air, Finley's hands were sweaty. He thought about his new friends hiding beneath the bricks. He couldn't let them get caught!

They came to the bridge. The police and the slave catchers were there. They held long, old fashioned guns.

Finley gulped. His stomach twisted up in knots. How could he act normal when he was so scared?

Then Fiona started talking. Her voice was loud, as usual. She did not sound afraid. "When we get to the Sweets Shop, I am going to make home-made apple pie. I'm going to pick the most crispy, juicy apples and sprinkle cinnamon and sugar all over them."

"Sounds delicious," the wagon driver said.

Finley looked at the men guarding the bridge. They were listening to Fiona. They looked hungry!

"My brother, the Cupcake King, makes the sweetest cupcakes. They are covered in frosting so yummy, you'll have to lick your fingers!" she said, laughing.

"We make the best desserts ever," Finley joined in. "Sticky taffy, gooey cookies, crunchy toffee, and fudge that melts in your mouth!"

"I must visit your Sweets Shop!" the driver said.

The wagon rumbled across the bridge. Finley was pretty sure he could hear the guards' stomachs rumbling too. But no one tried to stop them.

When they reached the other side of the bridge, Finley wiped his forehead. "Whew! That was close!"

"You did great," Fiona said.

Finley tapped his hearing aid. "What? I can't quite hear you."

Fiona scrunched up her face. "You heard me just fine!"

When they rounded a bend in the road, the kids helped the driver move the bricks out of the wagon.

Everyone climbed out. Harriet wiped the brick dust off her skirt. "You two helped me conduct my passengers past one of the most dangerous parts of the journey. Thank you!"

"Will you make it to freedom?" Finley asked. "Please say you'll make it!"

Harriet smiled. "I will make this journey nineteen times. I will lead over 300 slaves to freedom. I was the conductor of the Underground Railroad for eight years, and I can say what most conductors can't say: I never ran my train off the track and I never lost a passenger."

"Wowza," Fiona said.

"Did you ever get tired?" Finley asked.

"Of course! But I never let that stop me from helping my people. In fact, when the Civil War breaks out, I will be a spy for the Union army. I know all the secret places of the South, so I can report the location, size, and movements of the Confederate army without being seen."

"A real spy!" Finley's eyes widened.

Harriet laughed. She hugged Finley and Fiona. "I must continue on my journey now. Remember, every great dream begins with a dreamer. You two can change the world!"

The woods began to whirl and shake and spin.

Finley and Fiona tumbled through the side door of the Sweets Shop.

"It's about time!" Tick Tock squawked.

"Welcome back," Mom said.

"What did you learn?" Dad asked.

Finley and Fiona looked at each other. "We learned that even when terrible things are happening, there are good people who will risk everything to fight for what's right," Finley said.

"And we want to be some of those people!" Fiona said.

About Harriet Tubman

Harriet Tubman was born into slavery around 1820 in a one room log hut on a plantation in Bucktown, Maryland. Slaves were not allowed to read nor write. A slave owner could sell his slaves any time he wanted. Slaves worked all day, six days a  week. Harriet began working when she was five years old.

When she was about twelve, Harriet refused to tie up a fellow slave for a beating. The slave owner struck her in the head with a weight. She was unconscious for days. For the rest of her life, she had terrible headaches and would fall asleep while walking, talking, or eating.
Harriet always longed for freedom. When she was twenty-two, she planned her escape. She used the Underground Railroad, a secret network of people who helped slaves escape

to freedom. She trudged through ninety miles of swamp and woodlands to reach freedom in Philadelphia.

Harriet knew she needed to help others find freedom, too. She rescued her parents, six brothers, and one sister. Over the next eight years, Harriet made nineteen trips, leading more than 300 slaves to freedom. If she had been caught, she would have been captured or killed. But she was smart and sneaky.

When the Civil War began in 1861, Harriet worked as a nurse and a cook for the Union Army. Soon the Union Army asked her to be a spy. She knew the swamps and forests and could travel without being seen. She reported the size, location, and movements of the Confederate army.

After the war, Harriet worked as a maid and a cook, selling pies and vegetables. She continued to help the poor, sick, and needy, welcoming them into her house. She helped establish a home in Auburn, New York, for homeless and elderly African Americans. On March 10, 1913, she died of pneumonia around the age of 93.

Comprehension Questions

1. What was the Underground Railroad?

2. How did Harriet get the runaway slaves safely across the bridge?

3. Name three interesting things about Harriet Tubman's life.

Websites to Visit

www.civilwar.org/education/history/
    biographies/harriet-tubman.html

www.professorgarfield.org/KBKids/video/
    kbs3076.swf

www.harriet-tubman.org/category/biography

Q. & A with Kyla Steinkraus

What was your favorite part of Harriet Tubman's story?

She was so brave in the face of great danger. She risked her own life to help other slaves reach freedom. Even though she was small, she was tough and strong. As a girl, she chopped down trees with her father.

What was the hardest part of writing about Harriet Tubman?

Having to choose only one scene of Harriet's life! She did so many amazing things and had some thrilling adventures. She even helped lead a successful raid for the Union Army. She believed in a woman's right to vote. She never quit fighting for others.

What do you think Harriet would say to kids today?

I think she would tell kids to be brave and fight for what is right. She once said, "Always remember, you have within you the strength, the patience, and the passion to reach for the stars to change the world."

About the Author

Kyla Steinkraus lives with her husband, two kids, and two spoiled cats in Atlanta, Georgia. She loves to read her kids stories about strong, brave women like Harriet Tubman. She also enjoys hiking, playing games, reading, and drawing. If she owned a Sweets Shop, she would only sell (and eat) chocolate!

About the Illustrator

Sally Anne Garland was born in Hereford England and moved to the Highlands of Scotland at the age of three. She studied Illustration at Edinburgh College of Art before moving to Glasgow where she now lives with her partner and young son.